A ValueTales® Treasury
Treasury
Stories for Growing Good People

Five New Imaginographies by
SPENCER JOHNSON, M.D.

Based on the original texts by
Spencer Johnson, M.D.,
and on the original texts by
Ann Donegan

ILLUSTRATED BY

DAN ANDREASEN

SIMON & SCHUSTER BOOKS FOR YOUNG READERS
NEW YORK   LONDON   TORONTO   SYDNEY

THANK YOU

Jon Anderson, Dan Andreasen, Margret McBride, Alexandra Penfold,
Paula Wiseman, Laurent Linn, Dorothy Gribbin, Lisa Ford,
Donna DeGutis, Faye Atchison, and Anne Bomke.

SIMON & SCHUSTER BOOKS FOR YOUNG READERS
An imprint of Simon & Schuster Children's Publishing Division
1230 Avenue of the Americas, New York, New York 10020
Copyright © 2010 by Spencer Johnson, M.D.
Portions of the text of this work were previously published in different form in:
The ValueTale of Louis Pasteur: The Value of Believing in Yourself by Spencer Johnson, M.D. © 1975
The ValueTale of Harriet Tubman: The Value of Helping by Ann Donegan © 1977
The ValueTale of Confucius: The Value of Honesty by Spencer Johnson, M.D. © 1979
The ValueTale of Helen Keller: The Value of Determination by Ann Donegan © 1976
The ValueTale of Will Rogers: The Value of Humor by Spencer Johnson, M.D. © 1977
For information about special discounts for bulk purchases, please contact
Simon & Schuster Special Sales at 1-866-506-1949 or business@simonandschuster.com.
The Simon & Schuster Speakers Bureau can bring authors to your live event.
For more information or to book an event,
contact the Simon & Schuster Speakers Bureau at 1-866-248-3049
or visit our website at www.simonspeakers.com.
Book design by Laurent Linn
The text for this book is set in Garamond.
The illustrations for this book are rendered in oil paints on shellacked Bristol board.
Manufactured in China
0610 SCP
2 4 6 8 10 9 7 5 3 1
Library of Congress Cataloging-in-Publication Data
Johnson, Spencer.
A ValueTales treasury: stories for growing good people / by Spencer Johnson ; based on
original texts by Spencer Johnson
and on the original texts by Ann Donegan ; illustrated by Dan Andreasen.
p. cm.
ISBN 978-1-4169-9838-9 (hardcover)
1. Biography—Juvenile literature. I. Johnson, Ann Donegan.
II. Andreasen, Dan. III. Title.
CT107.J585 2010   920.02—dc22   2009054126

Dedicated to the well-being of children around the globe

CONTENTS

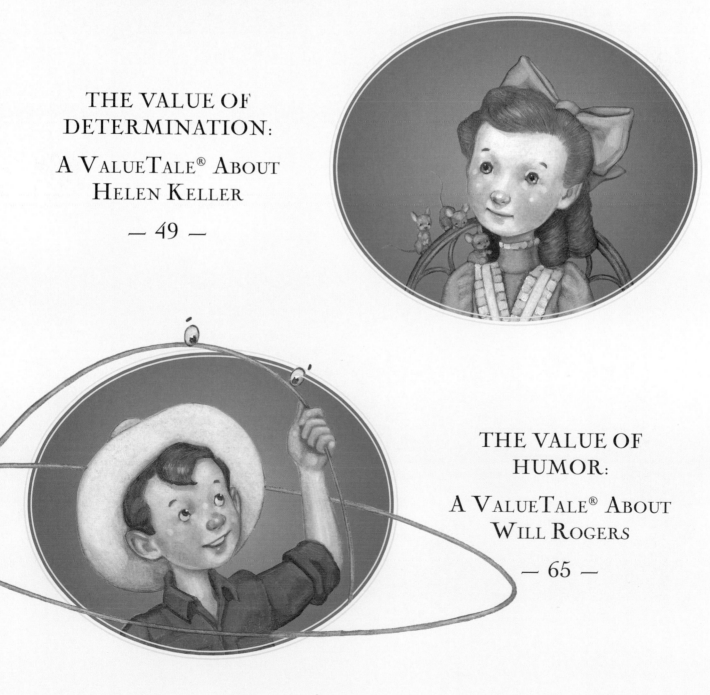

Hello, friend!

You're about to read a new kind of story called an Imaginography! Like a biography, an Imaginography is about real people and events, but it is told in a more fun and imaginative way.

You'll get to see how famous people grew into the good people they wanted to become—by listening to their True Voice, that special voice inside that gives us our best thoughts.

Each person's True Voice is unique and yours is too, depending on how you use your imagination.

I hope you like discovering the value of believing in yourself, helping, honesty, determination, and humor—and that you have fun growing up into the person you want to be!

Your friend,
SPENCER

THE VALUE OF

BELIEVING IN YOURSELF

A ValueTale® About
LOUIS PASTEUR

Hello. My name is Bee Lieve. I may look like an ordinary bee, but don't be fooled. You can imagine me as the True Voice of a real person named Louis Pasteur, who lived more than one hundred years ago.

I'm a fun way for you to see how Louis may have listened to himself—to his True Voice—that voice inside of each of us that gives us our best thoughts.

Now, when Louis was a little boy, long before he became famous, no one knew that invisible germs made people sick. One of the worst of these was called rabies. But as Louis grew up, he believed he could do what no one else thought he could.

What do you think Louis Pasteur believed he could do?

Well, to find out, let's begin our story together.

ONCE UPON A TIME there was a boy named Louis Pasteur. As he played with his toy soldiers, he wondered what he might do when he grew up.

"Maybe," he thought, "I might find a way to help people who are very sick."

That's when I buzzed in his ear: "Hello. My name is Bee Lieve. Believe in yourself, Louis, and you will be able to do more than you ever thought you could."

And Louis listened to me. He worked hard all through school, learning everything he could about medicine. All the while he repeated what he had heard from me, his True Voice.

"I believe I can," he said as he studied. "I believe I can find a cure for the invisible enemy called rabies."

Louis finished school and became a scientist. Many years later he began to work on finding a cure for rabies. But others made fun of him.

"How silly," they said. "If an enemy is invisible, then no one can find it."

Sometimes Louis became sad. "Maybe I can't," he admitted to himself. But then he heard a voice the laughing children did not hear.

"Remember," I told him, "when you believe in yourself, you can do more than you might think."

Louis listened to himself, smiled, and went back to work.

Years after people laughed and poked fun at Louis Pasteur, a little boy in a land far away was laughing and poking a stick at a poor sick dog. The boy's name was Joey. He wasn't really a cruel little boy. He just liked to tease, as some children sometimes do. But this was not a good idea. Unlike most dogs, who are friendly, this dog was so sick that white foam was coming from his mouth.

Do you know what was wrong with the dog?

The dog had rabies! If you were able to look inside the dog with a very powerful microscope, you would see the germs that were making him sick—and mad!

All of a sudden the dog bit Joey, and the germs that were hiding in the dog traveled into the little boy. Joey became very sick, and his parents worried. Everyone knew that anyone who was bitten by a dog with rabies would most surely die. All Joey's mother could do was comfort him.

But then one day she heard some very exciting news. "A scientist says he has found the invisible enemy that causes rabies—and maybe a way to cure it!" she exclaimed.

Joey's father hired a carriage with four fast horses. "Let's go!" shouted the coachman. "We haven't a second to lose!"

"Hurry!" said Joey's mother as the horses galloped.

"Hurry!" pleaded Joey's father.

Even the trees seemed to whisper: "Hurry! Hurry! Faster! Faster!"

Joey and his parents were on their way to see the man who may have found a cure for rabies.

Can you guess who the man was?

It was Louis Pasteur! Yes, the man who listened to me, his True Voice, and came to believe in himself. He had done what he believed he could do.

"Dr. Pasteur," Joey's mother asked, "can you help us?"

I smiled as I heard Louis say, "I believe I can!"

Louis explained, "You see, what we have always thought to be an invisible enemy isn't really invisible at all. Rabies is caused by a tiny bug called a germ that is so small that it can only be seen with a microscope.

"Once I discovered the germ that causes rabies, I was able to find a way to fight that enemy. I have invented a new medicine."

"Will it work?" groaned Joey, who was now very sick.

Do you think Louis's medicine will work?

"Think of my medicine as Magical Soldiers," said Louis, "with bright eyes that can see in the dark. They, like the germs, are too small for us to see with our eyes. But these tiny soldiers will travel down through a needle and go inside of you and find the enemy. Then they will do battle with the germs until they destroy them all."

Despite his fear of needles, Joey listened to *his* True Voice—his own best thoughts. It told him he needed to be very brave. It was the only way to get the medicine into his body to do battle with the germs. His parents were also very brave because they knew that no one had ever tried this before.

"Will it be dangerous?" worried Joey's father. "Are you sure your medicine will work on a little boy?"

"I believe it can," said Louis Pasteur, and he gave Joey his shot.

Louis's Magical Soldiers, called the rabies vaccine, went to work and began to battle the rabies germs. By now there were millions of them inside Joey, and it was a very fierce battle indeed. But the medicine was more powerful than the germs, and they were soon outnumbered and destroyed.

What do you think would have happened if Louis had not believed in himself?

When the last of the enemy had been beaten, Joey felt better—so much better that he jumped out of bed and danced around in a circle with his mother and father and, of course, Louis Pasteur.

I danced too!

I buzzed in his ear. "Louis, you really do believe in yourself."

Louis smiled and was very happy.

Are you *happy when you believe in yourself?*

When he was much older, Louis was invited to England for a special meeting of important doctors. As Louis arrived, all of the doctors stood up and cheered.

Louis said humbly, "The Prince of Wales must be arriving nearby."

"No, Louis," I buzzed, "they're cheering for you and all of the wonderful discoveries you have made."

Today we all still benefit from Louis Pasteur's belief in himself. He discovered other germs and found more ways to make things—including the milk you drink every day—safer for people.

That's right! He discovered a way to keep germs out of milk through a process that's called *pasteurization*.

Can you find Pasteur's name on your milk container?

As you can see, our story ends happily. Now you might want to think about *yourself*. Does believing in yourself make sense to you?

What you may want to do in your own life, of course, may be different from what Louis did. Whatever you choose, you may discover that when you believe in yourself, in big and small ways, you can be happier too—just like our good friend Louis Pasteur.

LOUIS PASTEUR (1822–1895)

LOUIS PASTEUR was a real person and the historical events in this ValueTale® really happened.

He was born in Dole, France, in 1822, the son of a tanner, in the province of Jura. In 1847 he earned a doctorate at the École Normale Supérieure in Paris.

As a chemist, and later as a bacteriologist, Pasteur did more than any other person of his time to further medical progress. However, because he was not a medical doctor, many leading physicians of the 1800s jeered at his theories. He ignored their scorn because he believed so strongly that bacteria, or germs, did indeed exist and that they could cause disease. He continued to work in his own way, having faith in himself, and eventually made progress against silkworm disease, anthrax, and rabies.

Pasteur's rabies vaccine was first administered to nine-year-old Joseph Meister on July 6, 1885, after the boy was bitten fourteen times by a rabid dog. Pasteur used his vaccine at some personal risk since he was not a licensed physician and could have faced prosecution for treating the boy. Pasteur the scientist hesitated to give his untried rabies vaccine to the boy. However, when two physicians pointed out that the boy would surely die without the vaccine, and Pasteur might just have the answer, Pasteur went ahead with the treatment. It proved to be a spectacular success, with Joseph Meister avoiding the disease, and Pasteur was hailed as a hero. Meister later became a gatekeeper at the Pasteur Institute. He stayed there, loyal to Louis Pasteur, for the rest of his life.

Pasteur also invented a process to keep milk from spoiling. Originally the process consisted of heating the milk to 140° F for thirty minutes, then cooling it quickly and keeping it in sealed, sterile containers. This process, called pasteurization, is used today in various ways to keep milk free from germs.

While Pasteur certainly believed in himself, he remained a quiet and humble man until his death in 1895. In his later years, he was amazed and amused by the fuss that people made over him.

Louis Pasteur founded the Pasteur Institute in Paris. Today there are twenty-four Pasteur Institutes around the globe that remain important centers for the study of infectious diseases and molecular genetics.

Because Louis Pasteur believed in himself and found the germs that caused diseases, he changed medicine forever and benefited people all over the world.

For more information on Louis Pasteur visit your local library, the website pasteurfoundation.org, or the Library of Congress online at loc.gov.

THE VALUE OF

HELPING

A ValueTale® About
· HARRIET TUBMAN ·

Hello! Here I am . . . up here in the sky. You can call me Starry! I've seen a lot from up here, but nothing like the story of a little girl named Harriet, who became famous for helping people.

You can imagine me as her True Voice—the voice inside her that Harriet learned to listen to even when things were difficult. Of course, she couldn't really see me, but perhaps she imagined me as a star, as you will soon discover.

So, if you're ready, let's begin our story together.

ONCE UPON A TIME there was a young girl named Harriet. Harriet was born during a time when it was actually legal to own another person in certain parts of the United States. Harriet was a slave and she was forced to work very hard for the man who owned her. At harvest time Harriet and the other slaves picked corn late into the night. While they worked, they would often sing a song about the people of Israel who had been held captive as slaves in Egypt.

> *Go down, Moses,*
> *Way down in Egypt's land.*
> *Tell old Pharaoh,*
> *Let my people go.*

"I wonder if anyone will help us the way Moses helped the people of Israel escape from Egypt," Harriet would say.

The slaves would often whisper about places where black people could be free. "There aren't any slaves in the Northern states," said Harriet's father. "All the people there are free men and women."

"I want to go north, Daddy!" said Harriet. "I want to be free."

"You see that star up there," said her father, "the big one that never moves? That's the North Star. When you get older, you can go north. Just keep that star in front of you. It will take you to freedom."

That's where I come in! As Harriet looked at the real North Star, she imagined that she had a star inside her that would guide her. I became her True Voice, that special friend inside of each person that helps you listen to your own best thoughts.

As Harriet got older, her desire for freedom grew stronger. She heard stories about something called the Underground Railroad.

"What is the Underground Railroad, Harriet?" I asked her.

"It's a secret way to escape to freedom," she explained. "Some white people and black people help slaves travel along safe paths. The houses the slaves hide in are called 'stations' on the 'railroad.'"

Many slaves made it to freedom, but Harriet saw how slaves who were caught were brought back in chains. She was too scared to attempt it herself.

Instead, Harriet decided she would work hard baking pies and then sell them door-to-door to earn money. You see, if slaves could make enough money to give to their owners, they were sometimes able to buy their own freedom.

"Starry," she asked me, "how many pies do you think I'll have to bake to earn enough money?"

"I think we're getting closer, Harriet," I whispered. "Let's keep baking!"

Harriet listened to herself, smiled, and went back to work more determined than ever to secure her freedom.

While out selling her pies, Harriet met a woman who saw how determined she was to be free.

"If you want to escape," she said to Harriet, "I can send you to people who will help you along the way."

That's when I whispered to Harriet, "If you accept her help, it can get you to a place where you may be able to help other slaves."

Harriet thought a long time about whether she should attempt to escape. Harriet knew that there were people who were risking their own freedom in order to help slaves like her. But it would still be very dangerous.

Do you have people who help you in your life?

One day Harriet heard a rumor that her owner was going to sell her. Harriet made up her mind then and there that she was going to escape. She set out that very night and headed into the woods.

"Don't be afraid," I whispered to her. "Your daddy always said if you followed the North Star, it would take you north to freedom. You can do it. You're strong and you've got the courage to be free!"

Harriet needed her courage. She went on for fifteen more nights, struggling through the darkness. She tumbled into holes, and she tore her clothes on briars. In the daytime she hid in barns and cellars, because there were men out everywhere searching for runaway slaves. But all along the way she found people to help her. They passed her along from one helpful person to another until at last she crossed into the North.

Do you think Harriet will now be safe?

Freedom was as wonderful as Harriet had thought it would be. Harriet knew that she'd be safe if she remained in the North, but she couldn't help but think about the many slaves who didn't have their freedom. She soon joined the Underground Railroad herself so she could help others. Over the next ten years, Harriet helped so many slaves escape to freedom that people started to call her Moses.

"Look, Harriet," I pointed out. "There are posters offering money for your capture."

Harriet cried, "Starry, this one says I'm worth forty thousand dollars!"

Harriet was afraid of what could happen if she were captured, but she carried on.

Harriet found many other ways to help. When the Civil War erupted, she joined the Northern army and traveled to the South to act as a nurse for injured soldiers. She organized the local slaves to help spy on the Southern forces. She even acted as a spy herself and helped plan an attack on a Southern plantation that freed over 750 slaves.

When the war was over, even after all she had done, Harriet was only allowed to ride home lying on the floor of the train's baggage compartment.

"Starry, we have a long way to go before we're really free."

I was too sad to even answer.

When she got home, Harriet let people know about the terrible way she had been treated.

The newspapers spread her story and many people who read it became upset. Over time more and more people worked harder to make things better.

Today, thanks to the help of Harriet and others like her, many people are treated more fairly than before, but there is still much work to do.

Now as our story ends you might want to think about *yourself*. You may not face the same struggles in your life as Harriet, but whatever you do, you may discover that when you help people, in big and small ways, you can be happier too—just like our good friend Harriet Tubman.

HARRIET TUBMAN (C. 1820–1913)

HARRIET TUBMAN was born a slave in about 1820 in a small village called Bucktown in Dorchester County, Maryland. Harriet was the daughter of slaves. Her grandparents on both sides were brought to America from Africa sometime after 1725.

Very early in her life, Harriet witnessed the inhumanities of slavery. She personally endured hard labor and many beatings. Harriet was determined to be free, but she was careful to hide this fact from her white masters.

When she was fifteen, Harriet saw another slave trying to escape. She deliberately got in the way of her overseer. In a rage, the overseer struck her in the head with a two-pound iron counterweight. For months after this savage attack Harriet was near death, and this incident left her with a dent in her skull and with strange seizures, during which she would suddenly fall asleep. Still, her desire to be free was fiercer than ever.

In 1849 Harriet succeeded in escaping slavery by making her way to Pennsylvania, earning money so that she could try to get her parents out of the South. She soon became involved with the Underground Railroad, an elaborate network of routes and guides and hiding places that helped runaway slaves reach safety in the northern states.

Harriet soon became one of the most active "conductors," earning for herself the name of Moses. Despite wanted posters with her description hanging in most towns, and a reward offered for her capture of up to $40,000, she went on with her work.

She personally helped at least three hundred slaves escape. In the years immediately before the Civil War, Harriet became good friends with many prominent Abolitionists. When the war came, she volunteered her services, and she worked as a nurse, laundress, cook, and spy for the Union army in South Carolina.

Throughout her long life, Harriet continued to work for freedom and equality. When she was eighty, Harriet appeared on platforms with leaders such as Susan B. Anthony and Elizabeth Cady Stanton.

Harriet died on March 10, 1913. A bronze plaque on the Cayuga County Courthouse in Auburn, New York, is a tribute to this great American woman.

For more information on Harriet Tubman visit your local library, the website harriettubman.com, or the Library of Congress online at loc.gov.

THE VALUE OF

HONESTY

A ValueTale® About
CONFUCIUS

Hello, I'm Sage. You might expect me to say *whoo whoo* like most owls do. But I also ask *Where? When? How? What?* and *Why?*

I knew a boy who grew to become one of the most famous people in history because he was so wonderfully honest. *Who?* His name was Confucius. *Where?* He lived in China. *When?* Over two thousand five hundred years ago. *How* do I know it? That's easy, you can imagine me as his True Voice—the voice inside Confucius that helped him listen to his best thoughts and guided him on his path.

Confucius started his journey when he was not much older than you. *What* did he do? Well, let's find out together.

ONCE UPON A TIME in the Chinese province of Lu there was a little boy named Confucius. His father was an old man when Confucius was born, and he was happy to have a son late in life.

His father would often tell Confucius how proud he was of him and how certain he was that his son would grow into a wise and honest person. Confucius loved his father dearly.

But all too soon his elderly father died and it was very difficult for Confucius and his mother.

Confucius was sad but he was determined to become the man his father hoped he would be, and the person he himself wanted to become—a wise and honest man.

This is where I, Sage, come in. Of course Confucius couldn't really see me, but I'm a fun way to imagine him listening to that good voice inside him—his True Voice.

One day little Confucius wondered, "How do I become wise?"

I appeared and whispered, "Hello. My name is Sage. You have already begun. Ask yourself, *'What is true?'* In truth you will find honesty. And in honesty you will find the best answers."

Then Confucius said, "I like to read books because sometimes I find answers there."

"That is good," I replied. "But not all wisdom is found in books. You can also learn much by watching and listening."

And Confucius *did* learn by reading, watching, and listening. When the time came, Confucius got his first job tending cattle.

"How do I do it, Sage?" he asked. "I've never done that before."

"Ask yourself, *'What is true?'*" I whispered.

"Hmm," said Confucius. "Maybe I could find what is true by imagining how I would like to be treated if I were an animal, and then treat them in a similar way."

Confucius laughed at what he imagined, and realized he needed to find ways to do his job that were practical, and so he did. He took care of the cows the way he would have liked to be taken care of.

The cattle grew happy and healthy and multiplied, and the owner was so pleased that he gave Confucius a new job—measuring and selling grain.

On his first day selling grain to the townspeople, Confucius was given some advice from a dishonest seller.

"There's no need to put a full measure of grain into the bag. No one will be aware, and you'll make more money like I do."

But I whispered in Confucius's other ear, *"What is true?"*

Confucius smiled as he listened to himself. "I would like to be treated honestly," he said, "so I will be honest with others." Then he filled his sacks with a full measure of grain.

Do you think Confucius felt good when he was honest?

Word of Confucius's honesty spread and many people admired him. One day a wealthy man asked Confucius if he would become a teacher to his son. Confucius said that he would be willing to teach all who are interested in learning, but that he would only charge those whose fathers had the money to pay, while other children would be able to attend his school for free.

Confucius never shouted or scolded his students, but when they misbehaved, he would send them away. "I will not force anyone to listen to me," he would often say.

Do you think it is good to listen?

Confucius's fame as a great teacher spread, and he would often travel to give his lessons. In those days people traveled by foot, so Confucius would walk far and wide spreading his teachings.

Confucius gathered many followers, read in many libraries, and even studied music. He learned to play an instrument and how to sing more than three hundred songs!

Do you think it might be fun to learn to play music and sing?

Once on his travels, though, something terrible happened. Confucius came to a city where he was mistaken for a man who looked a little like him, but who was an evil bandit who had robbed the people before! The people of the city captured Confucius and threw him into a dark and dirty prison.

"You are an honest man, Confucius, and surely they will release you," I said to him.

Confucius smiled as he listened to himself. He trusted that his honesty would set him free.

And it did! Confucius's reputation for honesty had spread so far that people came from all over to speak up for him. The people of the city were so impressed that they let Confucius go.

"By your being honest," I said to Confucius, "others have gone out of their way to speak the truth about you."

Confucius's reputation grew so large that he was called back to his home province of Lu and made governor. There he put his teachings into practice by dealing with everyone honestly. Because the government dealt with them honestly, the people of Lu became more honest with each other, and Lu became a happier place to live.

By listening to his True Voice, Confucius not only made himself happier, but everyone around him became happier too!

Are you happier when you are honest,
and when people are honest with you?

THE VALUE OF

DETERMINATION

A VALUETALE® ABOUT
HELEN KELLER

Hello! Hello! Hello! As you can see, there are three of us. Our names are Sight, Sound, and Speech. We're the True Voice of a remarkable girl named Helen Keller.

You know, your True Voice is that voice inside you that gives your best thoughts. Helen was unlike most children because she could not hear or see or even speak.

We are going to help you discover how, in spite of all this, Helen went on to live a very happy and successful life indeed—because she knew the value of determination.

Close your eyes and plug your ears for just a few moments. Can you imagine what life might have been like for Helen Keller?

Well, let's discover that together.

Progress was slow and difficult. Helen had liked it when every-one had spoiled her. But Anne wasn't giving in to any of Helen's tantrums. She was going to help her change. Helen, however, was determined that she would not change.

"Helen, it's good that you are very determined," we would share with her. "But can you use your determination to discover what Anne is trying to teach you?"

"I will not," she answered us silently. "I want to do things *my* way!"

Helen didn't know that Anne was just as determined. Anne spent weeks having Helen touch things and then spelling their names in Helen's hand.

One day Anne took Helen to a well and pumped water on her hands. It was cool and wet. Then Anne spelled the word "water" on Helen's hand. And suddenly Helen understood!

"She is teaching me the words for things," Helen thought.

"That's right," we all responded. "There are many words to learn if you just have the determination to learn them."

Helen became very excited.

Can you remember how you felt when you
suddenly understood something?

Helen ran through the house touching a clock, and a lamp, and a chair, and her teddy bear. She touched the face of her mother and the mustache of her father. And with each new thing she touched, Anne would spell the word in her hand.

The more Helen learned, the more determined she became to learn more about everything she could.

"You're learning to hear with your hand," said Sound.

"And you're learning to see with your fingers," said Sight.

"Someday you may even learn to talk," added Speech, hopefully.

Helen was determined that she would. So she traveled with Anne to the Horace Mann School for the Deaf, and she set to work to learn how to speak.

Can you guess how Helen learned to talk?

When Miss Fuller, the school's principal, spoke to Helen, she placed Helen's hand on her mouth. As Miss Fuller spoke, Helen could feel how her principal's lips moved and how her tongue moved against her teeth. Helen learned to move her own lips and tongue in the same way.

"She's trying to make words," cried Speech. "She's learning to talk!"

Now Helen was finally listening to her True Voice, to herself—to her own good thoughts. She smiled often as she continued to learn how to speak more and more words.

Even though Helen was blind, she went on to learn how to read as well. She read books for the blind written in braille by running her fingers over raised dots that made up the words on the page.

She was so determined to learn all she could that Helen even went on to college, where she spent years studying and graduated with honors.

"We're so proud of you, Helen!" we whispered. "You are using your determination to accomplish so much!"

Can you see how determination might help you in your own life?

People were so impressed with what Helen had done that she became famous. Helen traveled all around the world speaking to many different groups of people—even kings, queens, and presidents wanted to meet her.

The most important thing that Helen did was to provide real inspiration. Through her determination, she helped people see that they too could overcome any difficulties they might have and live happier lives as well.

Today blind and deaf people have more resources than ever before, and through their own determination, they are doing amazing things.

Now, as our story ends, you might want to think about yourself. Could being more determined help you, too? You may face different problems than Helen, but whatever you choose to do, you may discover that when you know the value of determination, and use it in big and small ways, you can be happier too—just like our good friend Helen Keller.

HELEN KELLER (1880–1968)

HELEN ADAMS KELLER was born in Alabama in 1880. Helen was a healthy child, but at the age of nineteen months she was stricken by fever and became deaf, blind, and mute. Helen spent her early childhood in darkness, but when she was seven, her father learned that there might be help for Helen.

He and Helen's mother were delighted when that help arrived in the person of Anne Sullivan. Anne could understand Helen's problems, for she herself had been almost blind until, at the age of sixteen, an operation restored part of her sight. Anne saw that Helen, like many other handicapped children, had been greatly spoiled by parents who felt sorry for her. Anne insisted on discipline for Helen. Later Mrs. Keller was to say to her, "Miss Annie, I thank God every day of my life for sending you to us."

When Helen's father became ill, Helen did not want to ask him for more money for the special schools she needed. One of Helen's admirers came to her rescue and helped raise the funds to send her to school. That admirer was Mark Twain, the famous author. He was only one of the many people who were inspired by Helen Keller's determination, which enabled Helen to learn braille, to write, and even to speak. In 1904 she graduated with honors from Radcliffe College in Boston.

Anne Sullivan, who helped Helen Keller use the value of determination, died in 1936 at the age of seventy. After spending almost fifty years with Anne, Helen said of her, "A light has gone out that can never shine for me again."

But Helen now clearly knew the value of determination. She kept working to help others until her death in 1968. Helen wrote articles. She gave lectures for the American Foundation for the Blind, and she helped raise a fund of two million dollars for this foundation.

On Helen's eightieth birthday the American Foundation for Overseas Blind honored her by announcing the Helen Keller International Award for those who gave outstanding help to the blind.

A source of personal inspiration to many people, Helen Keller was invited to visit every president of the United States from her childhood on. Her determination was a source of amazement and inspiration even to presidents with all the challenges they must face.

To show how much she valued that determination, she once said, "The marvelous richness of human experience would lose something of rewarding joy if there were no limitations to overcome."

For more information on Helen Keller visit your local library, the website helenkellerbirthplace.org, or the Library of Congress online at loc.gov.

THE VALUE OF
HUMOR

A ValueTale® About
WILL ROGERS

Howdy, pardners, my name's Larry! Larry Ett. I may look like a rope, but you can think of me as the True Voice of Will Rogers, one of the most well-liked people in the whole world. He was born long ago in Oklahoma, way back before it was even a state.

Will was famous for making people laugh. He listened to his good thoughts—me—and I helped him to see what was funny, especially in difficult times. This made things better for Will and for the people around him. And your good humor can help *you*, too.

How? Well, let's find out together.

ONCE UPON A TIME there was a little boy named Will. He was much rowdier than his seven older sisters and spent all his time fooling around. Will loved to hang on to the tail of his pony as it swam down the river.

"You shouldn't be playing when you've got chores to do," scolded his father.

"Oh, dear. Whatever will become of Will," worried his mother.

As much as Will liked speaking in front of his classmates, he had a hard time studying. One day he decided to quit school and run away.

"This doesn't seem like such a good idea, Will," I whispered.

But Will was determined to become a real cowboy. He used me to practice his roping day and night. And he created jokes that made even the cows laugh.

As fun as life was on the ranch, Will worried about his future. "What's to become of me, Larry?" he asked.

"You've got the gift of humor, Will," I told him. "You just have to figure out how to make it work for you."

Will listened to himself, then smiled and began to think more about what he would do.

When he was older, Will went to the city. He decided to get up on stage to do his rope tricks and tell jokes. But Will did it in a way that no one else has ever done. He did it on a horse!

But the stage was so slick that the horse kept slipping. People thought it was pretty funny, but Will realized he could hurt his horse that way. So he decided to do the act all by himself.

What do you think Will did?

During his show, Will made a mistake and got himself all tangled up in his rope. At first he was embarrassed when people began to laugh at him.

"I look like a fool, Larry," he said to me.

"Use your sense of humor," I whispered back. "Make them laugh *with* you, not at you. You can begin by laughing at yourself."

Will thought quickly and said to the crowd, "A rope ain't so bad to get tangled up in, as long as it isn't around your neck!"

Then the crowd really started laughing. They loved that Will could poke fun at himself.

From that point on, people started coming from all over to see the cowboy who had such a good sense of humor.

Will became so famous that even Woodrow Wilson, the president of the United States, came to see him perform.

Will was worried. "Uh-oh, Larry, I've got jokes about the president in my act. What if he doesn't have a sense of humor about himself?"

I assured him, "You never tell jokes in a mean way. Just do your act. The president is a big enough man to be able to laugh at himself."

And sure enough, no one laughed louder than President Wilson.

Do you feel good when you are able to laugh at yourself?

Soon *everyone* wanted to hear more of Will Rogers's humor and to know what he thought about the things that were happening in the world. Will played the biggest theaters in New York. He made the most successful movies in Hollywood. He wrote columns that appeared in newspapers across the country. And he talked to many people through his radio show.

Will Rogers had become the most famous man in America because he made people laugh and think.

"Well, I sure didn't expect all this to happen, Larry," he said.

"Why not, Will?" I replied. "You've developed your sense of humor, and now you're sharing it with everyone."

Everyone liked Will, and Will liked everyone—because he saw the funny side of things and helped others to see it too. He was famous for saying, "I never met a man I didn't like." Will tried hard to understand other people. "It's great to be great," he would say, "but it's greater to be human."

Will Rogers's sense of humor not only made other people happy, it made Will much happier as well.

Today Will's work is carried on thanks to the work of the Will Rogers Institute. Founded after Will's death, it does all kinds of important research and helps educate people about health and fitness. Because Will was involved in the movie business, the institute raises much of its money in movie theaters.

Now, as our story ends, you might want to think about *yourself*. Could using your sense of humor help you, too? What you may want to do in your own life, of course, may be different from what Will Rogers did. But whatever you choose, you may discover that when you use your sense of humor, in big and small ways, you can be happier too—just like our good friend Will Rogers.

WILL ROGERS (1879–1935)

WILLIAM PENN ADAIR ROGERS, the youngest of eight children, was born on November 4, 1879, in his parents' ranch house in what was the Indian Territory that is now the state of Oklahoma.

His father, Clem, was one-eighth Cherokee and his mother, Mary, was one-quarter Cherokee. Even the name of the state where he was born, Oklahoma, was derived from American Indian words. (*Okla* means "red" and *homma* means "people.") Will later said, "My ancestors didn't come over on the *Mayflower*. They met the boat."

Will's mother died when he was only ten years old. It was a great loss to Will, who missed her gentle manner, sense of humor, love of music, and easy way with people—some of the strongest traits inherited by her son.

The fun-loving son of a prosperous father, Will had every chance for a good education. But as bright as he was, Will wasn't interested in any of the many different schools he attended.

Will Rogers always spoke with a distinct Western drawl and a total disregard for proper English. When Will is quoted in this book, his words are paraphrased into language that most people feel is more appropriate for today's children to learn. Will's wife, Betty, tried to encourage him to speak properly, but Will always felt that his down-home, honest drawl was at least partially responsible for his unique success.

More than anything else, though, it was Will's sense of humor that helped him succeed as a philosopher, columnist, movie star, radio personality, philanthropist, and human being.

Will loved to travel and he was a great promoter of two new modes of transportation: the automobile and the airplane. His friends included Henry Ford (who presented Will with the first Model A car). He was friends with most of the leading aviators of his time, including Billy Mitchell, Charles Lindbergh, and Wiley Post.

Will's life ended in 1935 on a flight around the world with Wiley Post. Their plane crashed in desolate Point Barrow, Alaska. The entire world mourned Will's death.

It was very risky to fly in those days. The airplane was just being developed. But Will had always been one to take risks. He once gave a friend the advice, "Go out on a limb. That's where the fruit is."

Will also took a chance when he poked fun at hypocrisy, smugness, and greed even if they occurred in the most famous and important people. He did so with a good sense of humor, however. And people from every level of society loved him for it.

It was Will himself who said, "You can judge a man's greatness by how much he is missed."

For more information on Will Rogers visit your local library, the website wrinstitute.org, or the Library of Congress online at loc.gov.

ValueTales® Treasuries

LOOK FOR THESE STORIES IN FUTURE VALUETALES® TREASURIES:

Abraham Lincoln and The Value of Respect

Eleanor Roosevelt and The Value of Caring

Ludwig Van Beethoven and The Value of Giving

Marie Curie and The Value of Learning

Christopher Columbus and The Value of Curiosity